Felicity the Dragon

Ruthie Briggs-Greenberg

TAYLOR TRADE PUBLISHING
Lanham • Boulder • New York • London

Published by Taylor Trade Publishing
An imprint of The Rowman & Littlefield Publishing Group, Inc.
4501 Forbes Boulevard, Suite 200, Lanham, Maryland 20706
www.rowman.com

Unit A, Whitacre Mews, 26-34 Stannary Street, London
SE11 4AB, United Kingdom

Distributed by NATIONAL BOOK NETWORK

British Library Cataloguing in Publication Information Available

Library of Congress Cataloging-in-Publication Data Available

ISBN 978-1-63076-062-5 (cloth : alk. paper)

ISBN 978-1-63076-063-2 (electronic)

♾ The paper used in this publication meets the minimum require-
ments of American National Standard for Information Sciences—
Permanence of Paper for Printed Library Materials, ANSI/NISO
Z39.48-1992.

Printed in the United States of America

Dedicated to
all the misfits
of the world.

Sad little Felicity,
not quite the dragon she
thought she should be.

No smoke from her nose,
no spikes on her toes,
and her wings were too tiny
to carry her hiney.

She thought dragons were

big,

mean,

and ferocious!

Felicity was small, and not very precocious.

Nothing Felicity did was what a dragon should do.

Well, that's what she thought, and she thought she knew.

She never played with
any of the others,
she always felt different and
thought others would shudder.

She was sitting alone as she often did near the moat of a castle where four children lived.

And suddenly a very small boy stumbled while playing.

He fell right in the moat where
Felicity was staying!

The children all yelled,
and screamed,
"Help us, please help!"
And without even thinking,
Felicity jumped right into the kelp!

Her hiney went straight
to the mud bottom floor,
then a big wave formed and
carried the small boy to shore!

And the children all yelled,
but this time for joy,
and they said to sad Felicity,
"Thanks for saving the boy!"

And slowly, Felicity started to smile,
and the children said,
"Please, won't you stay
and play a while? "

And Felicity felt something new,
something different and right,
she felt useful and glad,
and her heart felt so light!

No longer sad she was
different and small,
Felicity had given to others,
but she gained the most of all.

And the gladness she felt
came from suddenly knowing
that her heart had reached out
and left others glowing.

The End